Missing!

Roderick Hunt • Alex Brychta

OXFORD
UNIVERSITY PRESS

Nadim had a hamster.

He called it Jaws.

"Jaws is a funny name for
a hamster," said Biff.

Nadim put Jaws in his cage, but
he forgot to shut the cage door.

Jaws got out of the cage and
ran away.

Nadim saw the cage was open.

"Oh no!" he said.

Nadim was upset.

"Jaws has run away," he said.

The children looked for Jaws.

They looked and looked.

Biff looked under the sink.

Chip looked in the fridge.

Nadim looked under the
cupboard.

Nadim's Dad looked for Jaws.

He pulled up the floorboards.

"Maybe Jaws is down here,"
he said.

Then Chip had an idea.

"Let's get Floppy," he said.

"He can find Jaws."

Sniff, sniff, went Floppy.

Sniff, sniff! SNIFF! SNIFF!

"Look in here," said Chip.

Jaws was in the clothes basket.

He had made a nest.

"Look!" said Nadim. "You can
see why I called him Jaws."

Think about the story

Why is the hamster called Jaws?

Why was Nadim upset when he found that Jaws had run away?

Where did the children and Dad look for Jaws?

What would you do if you lost your pet?

Odd one out

Which two things don't begin with the same sound as the 'h' at the beginning of 'hamster'?

Useful common words repeated in this story and other books in the series. called can had he look looked said the under was

Names in this story: Dad Biff Chip Nadim Floppy